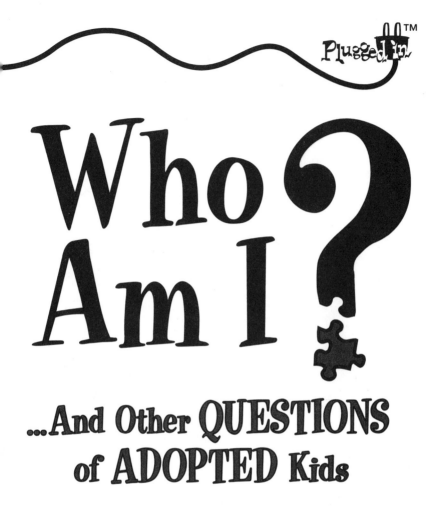

Plugged in™

Who Am I?

...And Other QUESTIONS of ADOPTED Kids

By Charlene C. Giannetti

Illustrated by Larry Ross

PSS!
PRICE STERN SLOAN

For Joseph and Theresa—C.G.

To Bud & Marcy and Lori & Nevin—L.R.

Text copyright © 1999 by Charlene C. Giannetti.
Illustrations copyright © 1999 by Larry Ross. All rights reserved. Published by Price
Stern Sloan, a division of Penguin Putnam Books for Young Readers, New York.
Printed in the United States of America. Published simultaneously in Canada. No part
of this publication may be reproduced, stored in any retrieval system, or transmitted,
in any form or by any means electronic, mechanical, photocopying, recording, or
otherwise, without the prior written permission of the publisher.

Library of Congress Cataloging-in-Publication Data

Giannetti, Charlene C.
Who am I? : —and other questions of adopted kids / by Charlene C. Giannetti ;
illustrated by Larry Ross.
p. cm. — (Plugged in)
Summary: Discusses various issues connected with adoption, such as the meaning of
adoption, the reasons why birthparents give up a child, and the search for birthparents.
1. Adopted children Juvenile literature. 2. Adoption Juvenile literature.
[1. Adoption.] I. Ross, Larry, ill. II. Title.
III. Series: Plugged in (New York, N.Y.)
HV875.G54   1999   362.73'4—dc21
99-41876
CIP

ISBN 0-8431-7529-X (pb) A B C D E F G H I J
ISBN 0-8431-7556-7 (GB) A B C D E F G H I J

Plugged in is a trademark of Price Stern Sloan, Inc.
PSS! is a registered trademark of Penguin Putnam Inc.

CONTENTS

CHAPTER ONE
What Does It Mean to Be Adopted?

Do you remember the first time you learned that you were adopted?

Maybe you feel like you have always known. Maybe you grew up watching *Sesame Street* and got excited when Susan and Gordon adopted baby Miles or maybe you had a favorite picture book. If you were born in Korea or China, then perhaps *Katie Bo* or *China Eyes* was the story your parents read to you over and over again. However it happened, at some point you learned that adoption was another way a family is started. And that this is how you came to belong to your family.

You probably went through many years in grade school knowing that you were adopted but not really examining what that meant. What really mattered was that you were living in a family that loved you and took care of you. How you arrived in your family seemed unimportant.

Now that you are an adolescent, no doubt you're beginning to have other questions about yourself and your adoption. Yes, you came into this world just like every other child. But what happened to the people who created you and gave birth to you? What happened to the woman who carried you inside her body for nine months?

You are developing more sophisticated reasoning powers. You are moving from being a concrete thinker, where everything is either black or white, to being an abstract thinker, where many things are in shades of gray. The simple story of your adoption that you took for granted as a small child may no longer satisfy your inquisitive nature. You want to have a better understanding of why you were adopted. Why wasn't it possible for you to stay with your birth-family?

You're also much more self-aware—you think more about the person you are right this minute and the kind of person you will be a few years from now. Naturally, you think more about the two people who gave birth to you. Wondering what you will look like as a grown-up also raises questions about your birth-parents. What did they look like? That's probably very important to you. A study of 881 adopted children ages twelve through eighteen found that 94 percent of them wanted to meet their birthparents "just to find out what they look like." So if  you've had similar feelings, rest assured; you're not alone.

Undoubtedly, there are other things you are wondering about concerning your adoption. One purpose of this book is to assure you that it's okay to be curious about adoption. It's okay to ask questions and look for answers. And it's natural for you to be feeling this way now.

How much do you want to know about your adoption? Sometimes kids refrain from asking questions, worried that they might hurt their parents' feelings. That's not usually the case. Most adoptive parents, in fact, understand their children's curiosity and expect them to ask questions. Your parents may even have given you this book to encourage you to talk with them.

Hopefully the information here will answer some of your questions, or help you to go about finding answers. You can think of this book as a guide to help you learn more about who you are.

 # EXPLAINING ADOPTION

What is adoption?

Adoption is a legal process—one that transfers parental rights and obligations from the birthfamily to the adoptive family. In simple words, that means that your parents—your adoptive parents, not your birthmother or birthfather—are the people who are legally responsible for your care and well-being. It also means that you have all the same rights and privileges that a biological child has. If you have brothers who are the biological children of your parents, their legal rights and your legal rights are exactly the same.

Each year more than 120,000 adoptions take place in the U.S. Another 10,000 children are adopted from other countries and come to live in the U.S. That's a lot of people. In fact, there are now more than six million adopted people (sometimes called adoptees) living in the U.S. When you think about all the birthparents who decided to let their children be adopted, and all the adoptive parents who decided to adopt those children, you can see how we're talking about a huge number of people. If you were to add grandparents into the mix, you would discover that about 20 percent of the population in the U.S. is directly involved in adoption.

Today most kids first learn about adoption from friends who were adopted, like you. "My friend was adopted and she thinks it's for the better because she has a family who loves her and cares about her," explained an eleven-year-old girl. "She doesn't think it's any big deal or anything to hide." You probably don't think it's unusual to talk about your adoption with your friends. But it hasn't always been this way. Far from it. It's only within the last fifteen years that people have been talking openly about adoption.

For more than forty years beginning in the mid-1940s, virtually all adoptions were handled by agencies in a confidential manner. These were the days before Madonna, Jodie Foster, and others made single motherhood acceptable. In 1949, for instance, the unmarried actress Ingrid Bergman, already famous for her role opposite Humphrey Bogart in the movie *Casablanca*, had a child and nearly saw her career destroyed.

Before 1973, a woman faced with an unplanned pregnancy also didn't have the option of a legal abortion. A pregnant, unmarried woman would often visit an adoption agency and ask the social workers to find a home for her child. In most cases, these birthmothers had no voice in selecting the adoptive parents.

Agencies used to "match up" adoptees and adoptive parents based on physical characteristics and ethnic background. They reasoned that if the parents and children looked alike, no one would have to know that the children had been adopted. The goal was, on the surface at least, to create a family that looked like a biological family. Adoptive parents, in fact, were encouraged to hide the facts of the adoption from their children as well as from the outside world.

This attitude which encouraged secrecy harmed

many adoptive families. Some children grew up never knowing about their adoptions. When they did find out, they were shocked, hurt, and angry that their parents had hidden such important information from them.

By the mid-1980s, with abortion legal and the embarrassment of single motherhood gone, attitudes changed. Birthmothers who decided on adoption did so with the understanding that they could take a more active role in deciding where the baby went. Agencies began to allow birthmothers to choose adoptive parents through written profiles or, in some cases, through face-to-face meetings. Still other birthmothers wanted more say and decided to go through what is called an independent adoption—where birthmothers choose adoptive parents without the help of an agency.

This new openness soon affected the adoptive family, too. Parents were encouraged to tell children at a young age about their adoption. Back in the 1940s, there were no books on the subject. Now there are dozens of books to help prospective adoptive parents, as well as many picture books for children with adoption-related stories.

Making the adoption process more open has been a very positive thing. Everyone involved—the child, the birthparents, and the adoptive parents—has benefited. You are very fortunate that your adoption occurred in this new, more open time. Why? For one thing, you may be able to receive updated medical information from your birthparents. If, for example, you develop migraine headaches, it would help your doctor to know whether or not this was something that ran in your birthfamily.

There are many other reasons why the timing of your adoption was lucky, and those will be covered in a later chapter.

ADOPTION IS FOREVER

When your parents told you about your adoption, you probably learned that your birthmother couldn't take care of you and decided that the best solution was to let you be adopted, and then you came to live with your parents. Sounds very easy, doesn't it? But how adoption works is actually very complicated. At each step along the way, the law provides certain safeguards to make sure that all those involved in the adoption—the child, the birthparents, and the adoptive parents—have their rights protected.

How were your rights safeguarded? Your most important right was to be placed in a good home. Your parents, like all parents who hope to adopt, had to go through a process called  a home study. A social worker licensed by your state interviewed your parents about their desire to adopt a baby. He or she came to visit them in their home and spent time talking with them. As part of the home study, your parents filled out papers about their background and answered many questions. This let social workers understand that they would be good parents. They also had to submit medical and financial information to prove they would be physically and financially able to take care of you.

All of this might seem intrusive. But adoption officials take their jobs very seriously. They want to make sure that children are placed in homes where they are properly cared for. Couples who have biological children never go through this process. So, you might say that your parents passed a fitness test that most parents never have to take. Also, because the adoption process is lengthy and complex, particularly when the child is from a foreign country, only those adults who are truly serious about adopting actually follow through.

How were your birthparents' rights protected? Your birthparents needed the right to come to a decision about adoption carefully and calmly. If your birth-mother went to an adoption agency, a social worker made sure that she received counseling. During her sessions, she would have had an opportunity to think about all her choices. What were those choices? Well, she could have kept you and raised you, with or without the help of your birthfather. She could have had an abortion. Or, she could have arranged to find a family that would give you a good home.

If your birthfather knew about your birthmother's pregnancy, he may have helped her reach a decision. But often, birthmothers have to make the decision on their own. That's why receiving counseling through an agency or independently is so important.

Once your birthmother decided on adoption, she was asked to sign a special document called a consent form. If your birthfather was known, then he was asked to sign this paper, too. This signing probably happened several days after you were born. (In some states, however, birthmothers are allowed to sign before giving birth. This is called *preconsent*.) After this consent paper was signed, your adoptive parents were able to take you home.

If you were born in a foreign country, how did your parents find you? Sometimes U.S. adoption agencies cooperate with agencies abroad. These foreign agencies let the U.S. agencies know which children are available for adoption. When your parents were told about you, they probably received a photograph and some information about you and your birthfamily. Many people who have adopted babies from other countries talk about how they "bonded" with their new baby as soon as they saw the child's picture.

In the United States, after a birthmother has signed the consent form, she is given a certain amount of time to reconsider her decision. This is her right. The time frame differs from state to state, from as little as 72 hours to 90 days after birth. (In many foreign countries, however, the consent takes effect from the time the birthmother signs it.) This waiting period is meant to protect the birthmother, to give her time after the birth of the child to reflect on her decision to make an adoption plan.

How were the rights of your adoptive parents protected? In the U.S., after the waiting period expired, then your birthmother no longer could change her mind. Your parents were assured that you would remain with them. They still had to wait a certain amount of time to finalize your adoption. (Depending upon the state, that period varies from a few days to as long as six months.)

How was your adoption finalized? Your parents were given a date and time to appear in court. The judge reviewed all the adoption papers and may have asked your parents some questions. Your parents received something called an adoption decree, a legal paper which officially made them your parents. Later on, they received an amended birth certificate naming them as your parents. No doubt your parents were thrilled to have your adoption finalized. They may have turned the day into a celebration, inviting over family and friends to share their joy. Maybe you've even seen photographs of this special day.

Once your adoption was finalized, you became a permanent member of your family. Even if years later one of your birthparents searched for you and found you, he or she would not be able to take you away from your family. Truly, adoption is forever.

I'M DIFFERENT; I'M ADOPTED

In some ways, adoption makes you seem different. That feeling can be hard to deal with during adolescence when you are often trying so hard to fit in with your friends. The last thing any adolescent wants is to stick out. If the truth be told, it can be very uncomfortable when people first discover you were adopted. Have you had any of the following experiences?

- *Your teacher assigns you a class project to construct your family tree. While the other students attack the work with enthusiasm, your reaction is confusion. Which family tree are you supposed to illustrate, your adoptive one or your biological one? And how will you detail your birthfamily when you don't know who they are? "I was angry when my science teacher gave us a family tree assignment," said one thirteen-*

year-old boy. "She told me I could write a paper instead. Didn't she understand that that would make me feel even more left out?"

- In science, you are studying genetics. During a classroom discussion, the students talk about physical characteristics and personality traits they have inherited from their family. You have nothing to contribute to the discussion and so remain silent. "I was afraid the teacher would call on me," confessed one fifteen-year-old girl. "Then what would I say?"

- You are out shopping with your mother and the young salesperson ringing up your purchases remarks that you two look nothing alike. Your mother just smiles. You used to be able to laugh at such comments. Now you find them embarrassing.

- You have a fight with one of your best friends and you both say some hurtful things. But you are left speechless by her last insult: "You don't even know who your real parents are." Besides being devastated that she would say something so awful, you realize that she's right.

- At a sleepover party, one of your friends finds an astrology chart in a teen magazine. All the other girls know the hour and minute they were born and so have no difficulty figuring out their horoscopes, but you don't and it makes you feel weird. "My mother doesn't know the time of my birth and somehow not

knowing such a simple fact has always bothered me,"
said a thirteen-year-old girl.

Even if you have never thought much about your adoption, chances are, if you were placed in one of the situations described above, you might look at yourself in a whole new light. The facts of your adoption may seem unfair to you. Not to be able to look at your parents, siblings, aunts, uncles, cousins, and grandparents for a clue as to how tall you will be or what your nose will eventually look like has to be frustrating. At times you may even become depressed or angry about your situation. Why should you be denied information that just about all your friends take for granted?

You had no say in your birthmother's decision. You also had no control over which family became your own. Now, when you would like to learn more about your birthfamily, the law prevents you from obtaining any of that information. How can any of this be fair?

Well, it's not fair. There's no denying that. But lots of things are unfair. So while being adopted does matter, it doesn't have to rule your life. How you understand and accept your adoption will affect not only your own attitude but the attitude of others.

Sometimes people don't believe that adoption is normal. They say negative things about adoption because they just don't know any better. Once you educate yourself, you can use what you have learned to set other people straight.

There are some warped ideas surrounding adoption, ideas that are repeated so often that people begin to accept them as fact. For example, some people really and truly think all adopted children feel strange because they were adopted. That's just not true. Listen to eleven-year-old Ellie, who says adoption is just fine with her. "People ask me what it feels like to be adopted," she said. "I tell them it feels normal."

How do people get wrong ideas about adoption? Often the media is to blame. If a TV show or movie presents adoption in a negative way, that's what people will believe. Often the people writing these stories are well-meaning but misinformed.

Some adoptive-parent groups work to help people who write for TV and the movies understand adoption better. They write to movie and TV producers, magazine and newspaper writers, even to those who create greeting cards, to point out misleading and hurtful ways adoption is portrayed. These groups have had much success. The movie *Problem Child* is about a couple who adopt a nine-year-old boy who always gets into trouble. There were many negative comments about adoption in the movie. At one point the adoptive mother says she doesn't wear second-hand clothes and questions her decision to take in a second-hand child. Another time someone recommends giving the boy back, saying his birthparents probably came from the loony bin. Many adoptive parents were upset over the movie and they wrote letters to the producers. Their protest worked. When the sequel, *Problem Child II* came out, all references to adoption were removed.

Another time, adoptive parent groups objected to

a greeting card. The outside of the card said: "I can't believe anyone as smart and beautiful as I am would have a brother like you." Inside, the card said: "You were probably adopted." The group complained and the company discontinued the card.

Education is the key to changing people's attitudes. You can start with your own social circle of friends. Sometimes you need to correct their language. Do so in a tactful way so that you don't harm your friendship. For example, ask them to say "birthparent" rather than "real" parent. And "made an adoption plan," instead of "gave you up," or "put up for adoption," to explain your birthparents' decision.

Many adoption agencies have social workers who visit schools and talk with teachers and students alike to enlighten them about adoption. If you think such a talk would be good at your school, talk with your parents about suggesting it to the parents' association.

But you can do some educating on your own. If someone makes a negative comment to you about adoption, that's your chance to hit them with the facts. What follows is a list of some common myths about adoption and why they remain just that—myths.

Myth #1
Adoption makes you different from your friends.

Adoption means you came to your family by a different route. But, if you stop to think about it, adoption doesn't make you all that different from any of your other friends. Here are some ways you are like your friends who were not adopted:

You were born. Everyone is born. Everyone starts out with biological parents. Most children end up staying with these birthparents, but some do not. Your birthparents decided on adoption for you and you came to live with your adoptive parents. You may have friends who, because of divorce or family circumstances, are not living with both of their biological parents.

You have unique talents. Sometimes people receive these gifts from their birthparents; sometimes they don't. You probably know someone who turned out to have an ability—musical, athletic, or academic—that could not be traced to anyone in the family. If you

 have a special capability for something, you may have inherited that aptitude from someone in your birthfamily, or you may have developed that interest after being inspired by one of your parents, a sibling, a teacher, or a special friend. Either way, the gift is yours.

You are responsible for your destiny. If adoption holds people back, then how do we explain the success of Steven Jobs, the founder of Apple Computer; the Rev. Jesse Jackson; Jim Palmer, Baseball Hall of

Fame pitcher; Dave Thomas, founder of the Wendy's food chain; actresses Halle Berry and Melissa Gilbert; or Gerald Ford, our 38th President? Many people go through life looking for reasons to fail. For some, being adopted becomes the excuse. In reality, you and your friends all start on the same square. How you advance on the game board of life, what you do with your talents and skills, how you handle setbacks and failures, depends upon you and you alone.

Myth #2
Adolescents who were adopted have more problems than adolescents living with their biological families.

Back in the 1960s, research studies were done on small groups of adopted adolescents who were patients at mental health clinics. Not surprisingly, people in these groups were found to have psychological problems. Unfortunately, some people who were out to prove that adopted people were unhappy used these findings incorrectly. They said that adoption was the reason— the only reason—these people had mental problems. That wasn't true. The reasons people seek out help for mental problems are far more complex. The damage was done, however. For more than twenty years, these studies were often held up as proof that adoption was harmful.

Finally, in the 1980s, several studies were done that challenged the notion that adoptees have more emotional troubles than nonadoptees. One study published by the Child Welfare League in 1985 followed adoptive families for nearly twenty-five years. It concluded: "Evidence suggesting that the adoptee has greater or more sustained difficulty with the tasks of adolescence was not found, indicating that adoptive status, in and of itself, is not predictive of heightened stress among adolescents." In plain language, that means that the group of adolescent adoptees were doing quite well—being adopted didn't make adolescence any more stressful for these kids.

Another study released in 1985 backed up those findings. The adopted kids who participated in the study were from a nonclinical—that is, "normal"—population. They were found to be "significantly more confident and view others more positively than their non-adopted peers."

One of the largest studies done of adoptees and their families was conducted by the Search Institute, which is based in Minneapolis. This project involved an in-depth look at 715 families who adopted infants between 1974 and 1980. Some of these families also had biological children, and these children filled out the survey, too. When the survey was conducted, between 1992 and 1993, these adopted infants were adolescents, ranging in age from twelve to eighteen.

The study found that the adopted adolescents had positive attitudes and high self-esteem. In fact, in some categories, the adopted adolescents scored higher than their non-adopted siblings. Here's a rundown of the findings:

- *79% of adopted adolescents said they had a good sense of who they are, compared to 77% for non-adopted siblings.*
- *86% said they were glad they were born (87% for non-adopted siblings).*
- *77% agreed with the statement, "I'm lucky to be me." (79% for the other group).*
- *72% said they had a good idea of where they were going in life. (Only 66% of the non-adopted group were as sure).*

So now whenever people who are ignorant about adoption make negative comments, you have the facts and the statistics to show them they're wrong.

Myth #3
Adopted adolescents spend all of their time brooding about their adoptions.

Far from it! The Search study found that only about a quarter said that "adoption is a big part of how I think about myself."

Anna, sixteen, who was born in Korea and brought to the U.S. by her adoptive parents when she was still an infant, agreed with that finding. "Right now I'm a teen and there are so many more things going on in my life that are more important," she said. "I just don't think about my adoption all that much."

Of course, adolescents' interest in adoption is apt to ebb and flow, depending upon what other events are occurring in their lives. You probably notice this yourself. Are there some days when you wonder about your adoption, and then weeks when it's the farthest thing from your mind? Congratulations! You're normal.

Myth #4
Being in an adoptive family is not as good as being in a biological family.

Old-time TV shows—like *Leave It To Beaver* or *Happy Days*—claimed to show the "perfect" family. You've probably watched some of them on cable. What did all these programs have in common? They presented the ideal family as one that was white, with a working father, a stay-at-home mother, and at least two children, who were biologically related.

The dictionary defines "family" as "a social unit consisting of parents and the children that they rear." That definition says nothing about the members all being connected biologically. And indeed, today we are seeing many different kinds of families. We have families headed by one mother, one father, two mothers, two fathers, grandparents, or, as dramatized in the TV show, *Party of Five*, five children living together raising themselves.

The important element common to all of these

different families is that the members are committed to each other. They worry about each other, help each other, fight with each other, and have fun with each other. "Ellie is my sister," said Katie, fourteen. "Even though we didn't come from the same birthmother, we're sisters and we always will be."

All families—biological, adoptive, step, or otherwise—go through bad times. Sometimes there's a stretch when no one seems to get along. Illness, money worries, and having to move, all are situations that can temporarily turn a harmonious family into an unhappy one. We all know families that have suffered real tragedies. What made the difference for those families that survived? Chances are it wasn't the fact that there was a biological connection. Rather, their loyalty to each other and to the family was what pulled them through.

Myth #5
Your adoptive parents aren't your "real" parents.

Giving birth to a child is just the beginning. The true test of parenting comes afterwards.

Your "real" parents are the ones who tuck you in at night, drive you to the mall on the weekend, nurse you when you have a fever, cheer at your soccer games, and hug you when  you're feeling bad. That's what "real" parenting is about.

FILLING THE HOLE LEFT BY ADOPTION

You have experienced a loss in your life, the loss of knowing your birthfamily. This loss is one that will never be made up. Even if you search for and find your birthfamily at some time in the future, you will never be able to make up for lost time.

But let's put the situation into perspective. Hardly anyone gets through life without experiencing loss. One of your friends may have lost a parent. Or perhaps you know someone who is living with his divorced mother and does not get to spend enough time with his father.

How will you cope with this loss? It is your choice

whether you will use it to motivate yourself or whether you allow it to get you down to the point where you ruin any chance of a happy future.

Can you look at this loss another way? Where there is a loss, there often is a gain. You may have lost your biological family, but you still gained a family that loves you and takes care of you.

Earlier I mentioned some famous people—Halle Berry, Melissa Gilbert—who were adopted. Perhaps they would have been as successful if they had grown up in their biological families. But who knows? Jake, thirteen, sees his adoption as helping to shape his character. "I think my past and my being adopted has a lot to do with what kind of person I am today. It hasn't always been happy times, but the tough times have made me a lot stronger and wiser person." Rebecca, also thirteen, agreed with Jake's assessment. "I am adopted and everyone likes me for who I am, not where I'm from," she said.

Adolescence is an important time in your life. These are years when you will make important decisions about your future. Your adoption shouldn't be seen as an obstacle to your success. If you have questions, find a knowledgeable, caring adult to confide in. Talk with friends who also were adopted. You might want to join a group of adopted teens where you can share your thoughts with other kids who understand what you are going through.

Professionals who work with adolescents like to call each young person "a work in progress." What does that mean? Well, picture your life as a large, blank canvas. Each day, through the choices you make, you add a little more color and definition. Right now adoption may occupy only a small corner of the canvas. A year from now, it may take up a larger part as you try to understand it better.

The important thing is that you are the artist. You are the one in control. You are the one holding the brush, choosing the colors, filling in the space. You, and only you, will create the final picture.

CHAPTER TWO
Why Did My Birthparents Give Me Up?

Are you curious about your birthparents?

If you said no, ask yourself the question again and be honest. As an adopted child, you quite naturally have questions. What do your birthparents look like? Where are they? What do they do for a living? Do they have other children, your half-brothers and half-sisters? Do they think about you on your birthday?

You may understand that your birthparents weren't able to take care of you and so they decided on adoption. But knowing that doesn't necessarily stop a little voice in the back of your mind from asking, "Why couldn't they take care of me?" When you are really feeling down, you may even think that there was something wrong with you that caused them to "give you up."

Just as all kids are different, some adopted kids are more curious than others about their birth. Are you a curious person by nature? Do you take things apart to see how they run? Are you always the first one to ask questions in class? If so, chances are you will also be very curious about your adoption.

Perhaps you are more laid back, and take much of what happens to you for granted. That's okay, too, and would probably explain why, up until now, you may not have thought about your adoption all that much. But becoming a teenager means you have reached a milestone in your life, a point where many special events are happening to you. If you are a girl, you may be wondering when you will get your period. If you are a boy, you may wonder when your voice will change. Lots of your friends can just ask their parents how they developed physically. Now, more than ever, you may be wanting answers that are just beyond your reach.

WHAT WERE THEY THINKING?

As a small child hearing your adoption story, you probably focused on what a happy event it was. Your adoption meant that you found yourself in a loving family with parents who could take good care of you.

Now that you are older, you are able to look at that story from a different perspective. In English class you may have studied characters and written about their "motivations," why they did the things they did. For example, in *Moby Dick*, Captain Ahab's motivation was revenge. The whale had cost him his leg and he was determined to retaliate. In *Little Women*, Jo loved books and wanted to become a writer. That motivation shaped her destiny, not only what she would do with her life, but also whom she would spend it with: not Laurie, her handsome, fun-loving neighbor, but Mr. Bhaer, the professor who shared her love of literature.

If you were an infant when you were adopted, you had absolutely no say in what was happening. All the decisions were made by your adoptive parents and your birthparents. Your adoptive parents' motivation was to create a family. That's simple enough. They did that by finding you. But your birthparents' motivation is unclear. They are the big mystery, and they aren't here to explain their actions.

You may not have access to your own birthparents, and your adoptive parents may not have many details about them. But many birthmothers have spoken out about their decisions. Through their words, we can begin to understand what motivates most birthparents (and possibly yours) to choose adoption.

What it all boils down to is this: most birthmothers want to do the best thing possible for the baby. That usually means providing a loving, stable, two-parent home. The following is from a letter written by one birthmother to her three-day-old son, whom she named Sean Christopher:

"I wanted to keep you very much, but I had to think of what was best for you. I knew I couldn't depend on your birthfather and I didn't want to take charity from family or friends. I also knew I could never live on welfare or any other public handout. You deserve the very best from life, Sean, and I wanted to make sure you'd have it.

"There was one other factor of major importance in my decision. I didn't want to raise you without a father. My father died when I was eleven, and it was the most devastating event in my life. I've never gotten over it, and I just couldn't see putting you through something like that. I wanted you to have two parents who would be there for you."

Another mother, who named her son Thomas, told the adopting couple:

"This baby didn't deserve to come home to a mother who wasn't ready for him and without a father. I was the only one who could help rearrange this situation, and though it hurt to do so, I have no regrets."

No doubt you've heard the phrase, "For your own good." Your parents probably use it way too often, as far as you're concerned, to explain why you need to eat healthy foods, visit the dentist, or get vaccination shots. You may rebel because you want to be able to decide on your own what is good or bad for you. As an infant, you were too young to make a decision about who would raise you, so others assumed that responsibility.

Now that you're older, you may feel angry, sad, confused, or hurt not only by the decision, but by the way it was made, without considering your feelings, too. These are all understandable emotions and you need to talk about them with your parents or with another adult.

TEENAGE BIRTHPARENTS

An overwhelming majority of birthparents were only teenagers at the time. In fact, your birthparents may have been your age or near your age when you were born.

Can you imagine yourself right now being responsible for a baby? Pretty scary, right? Taking care of an infant isn't like playing with a doll or having a pet. Babies need—and demand—constant attention, twenty-four hours a day. They cry for all sorts of reasons: when they're hungry, thirsty, too hot, too cold, have a wet diaper, or have sore gums from teething. Perhaps you know some  new mothers and fathers and have seen how tired and cranky they can be at times. That's because having a new baby in the house often means parents must sacrifice their own comfort for the baby's well-being.

The strain of parenting a newborn is difficult enough for two adult people. But parents who are grown-ups are mature enough to handle all the frustrations, fatigue, and worries. And they have many sources of support. They have each other and can share the parenting. One or both of them have jobs, so they can support the child and are able to pay a babysitter and have an occasional night out. And while the responsibilities are great, these new parents knew what they were getting into. They planned for this baby and knew they could handle the job. In fact, they were excited, ecstatic about parenthood.

Teenagers who find themselves facing an unplanned pregnancy are in a much different situation. Think about it for a minute: run over in your mind what your days are like—school, sports, social events. How would an infant fit into your routine? What would you have to change—or give up—in order to care for a new baby?

In most cases, the burden of responsibility for raising the child falls on the birthmother. School becomes more difficult for her, even in some communities where high schools arrange for teenage mothers to continue their studies. For a teenage mother, there's no time for any extracurricular activities like plays, marching band, or soccer. Even with relatives helping out, a teenage mother still has overwhelming responsibilities.

There's no time for just being a teenager. No  Friday nights at the movies or Saturday afternoons shopping with friends. Then there are the bigger questions of what college or career plans may have to be given up.

You can't drive or vote before you are a certain

age. In most states you have to be twenty-one before you can drink alcoholic beverages. These laws are made so that people will be mature enough to make serious decisions. Yet there are no laws preventing young people from becoming parents even though they may not be mature enough to handle the responsibilities. Some teenagers, however, come to that conclusion on their own. That's why they choose to find a family to raise their child.

When you get angry about your birthmother deciding on adoption, you probably don't even put yourself in her place. If you try to, it may be easier for you to understand her motivation—to make sure that you would have a loving, stable home with mature parents who have the time and energy to care for you.

DEALING WITH ABANDONMENT

You may agree that your birthmother's decision was the right one. She couldn't take care of you. Your adoptive parents could, and your birthmother's desire to have you grow up in a close, supportive family has worked out. You know that you are loved and wanted.

So why do you sometimes feel abandoned?

Because, in order for you to come to live with your parents, your birthparents had to let you go. And no matter how anyone—your parents, teachers, counselors, or even friends—try to soften the blow, the reality is a difficult one to deal with. Someone gave you up, abandoned you. Even worse, people tell you that your birth mother abandoned you *because she loved you.* You can't help but think, "If my birthmother truly cared about me, she should have understood that the best thing for me was to remain with her." In other words, part of you believes your birthmother's motivation should have been to keep you no matter what.

Some adoptees, even those who are happy with their parents, feel hurt when they think about being abandoned by birthparents. Sarah Saffian, who was adopted as an infant and located at age twenty-four by her biological family, wrote about her conflicting feelings in her book, *Ithaka.* "My love for my family did not preclude the pain of being surrendered," Saffian wrote. "I could still feel abandoned, even if the parents who adopted me were as good, or better, than my birthparents might have been."

Others are able to look at the issue more positively. "I grew up with a sense of, 'Wow! I'm so lucky! My birthmother sacrificed for me and I came into a family that wanted me so much,'" said Kathleen Sweeney Scheier, who works for MTV Networks. "I don't remember ever feeling abandoned or unloved."

You will have to deal with the issue of abandonment in your own way. But keep in mind two things. First, when your birthmother decided on adoption, she did not know you as a person. She was dealing with an unwanted pregnancy, not an unwanted child. Also, her decision was based on her own feeling that she was not ready to parent a child—any child, not just you.

In the end, the important thing is not the abandonment issue, but whether you have people today who love you and care about you and who will be there for you in the future.

FANTASIZING ABOUT BIRTHPARENTS

Most children, adopted and nonadopted, fantasize about their origins. Whenever you are fed up with the parents you have, you start imagining that somewhere out there are your "true" mother and father who will appear one day and take you away from your ho-hum life. Perhaps you picture these "real" parents as royalty, a king and queen from some faraway country where young people have no curfews, unlimited spending money, and no homework. Paradise!

Your long-lost father may be a famous soccer player and your mother a movie star whose new film just happens to have a part tailor-made for you. School will just have to wait.

Your nonadopted friends probably fantasize about being adopted so they can dream of glamorous "real" parents who will appear one day. Of course, these friends don't really have another set of parents out there. You do. It is possible (although unlikely) that your birthmother is a star who will come looking for you the way the comedian

Roseanne Barr did when she sought a reunion with her birthdaughter. So if you, from time to time, fantasize about glamorous, famous, 110–percent–perfect birthparents, it's totally understandable. It doesn't mean that you don't love and appreciate your parents. It just means that you are curious about who your birthparents are. It's also safer than actually finding them. When you fantasize, you get to write the script.

"As a little girl, I pictured fairytale characters— Cinderella and Prince Charming, Snow White and Prince Charming, Rapunzel and Prince Charming," wrote Sarah Saffian in her book. "As an adolescent, my thoughts turned to the celebrities du jour: Was Marie Osmond my birthmother? Was John Travolta my birthfather?"

Some adopted children get so caught up in fantasizing that soon everyone around them is a potential candidate for birthparent, whether famous or not. Walking down the street, a teenage girl adoptee sees a woman whose high cheekbones and curly auburn hair resemble her own. "Could she be my birthmother?" the girl wonders. Another time she notices a man whose smile looks familiar. "He has to be my birthfather," she thinks.

Have you ever heard of something called "selective perception?" That phenomenon occurs whenever we become so focused on one thing that it appears to be everywhere. For example, say you want to get your ears pierced but your parents won't let you. Suddenly, everyone you see, no matter where you go, seems to have pierced ears. In reality, the number of people with pierced ears hasn't dramatically increased. But because the matter has taken on such importance in your mind, you are "selectively" screening out everyone who doesn't have pierced ears. Your "perception," therefore, will be that everyone else but yourself has pierced ears.

The same events may occur when you become caught up in learning about your birthparents. When you spend a great part of your day wondering who they are and what they look like, it's natural that you will study everyone who crosses your path. Anyone who has the smallest resemblance to you becomes a possible candidate for your birthparent.

You are not going crazy. Virtually all adoptees become "parent watchers" in their quest to learn more about their background.

Of course all this fantasizing also provides you with a comfort zone. Fantasizing is safe. In reality, you probably aren't ready to meet your birthparents.

WHEN YOUR FANTASIES TURN DARK

While some adoptees imagine their birthparents as beautiful, rich, famous, and successful, other children see their beginnings in a darker light. They picture their original parents as losers—high school dropouts, drug users, prostitutes, even criminals doing time in jail.

"My birthfather was probably a druggie," said one fourteen-year-old boy who also admitted he was experimenting with drugs. Like father, like son? Was this boy using his birthfather to justify his own actions?

Don't fall into that trap!

Yes, there is scientific evidence of a hereditary connection with some behaviors and conditions. Take alcoholism, for example. If one of your birthparents was alcoholic, you do stand a greater chance of running into problems with alcohol. But it doesn't mean you are destined to become an alcoholic, too. Plenty of children who have alcoholic parents resist following that path. Your home environment, and the example set for you by your parents, can make a big difference.

THE GENETIC LINK

What specifically have you inherited from your birthparents?

Many things, including:

Physical characteristics. How you look—the color of your eyes, the color of your hair and skin, your height, body type, and many other physical features—is the result of your genetic makeup.

Health. Scientists now know that many illnesses are inherited. If someone in your birthfamily had breast or colon cancer, for example, you are at greater risk for contracting one of these illnesses than someone whose relatives are cancer-free. Adult-onset diabetes, heart disease, high blood pressure, all are illnesses that run in families.

Talents. Certain abilities—musical, athletic, mathematical—*may* be inherited, too. One adoptive father tells this story:

"One thing we knew about the birthmother was that she loved to ice-skate and had Olympic aspirations. She wanted our daughter to have lessons and we have honored her request. I'm glad we had this information because our daughter has definitely inherited her birthmother's ability and excitement for this sport."

Of course, these gifts are not always handed down. Another adoptive father had a different experience:

"The adoption agency told us our son's birthfamily was musically talented. In fact, the birthmother requested that we make music a part of his life. So far we have been through the piano, guitar, and trumpet with no success. Musical talent may run in his birthfamily, but somehow, he was skipped!"

The main thing to keep in mind is that you are unique. You are a one-and-only mixture of whatever biological traits you have inherited from your birthparents and all the behaviors and knowledge you have gained from years of living with your adoptive parents. You are, quite simply, special. There is no one like you.

MAKING YOUR OWN CHOICES

You have inherited many things from your birthparents. But the choices they made were their own, not yours. You are not destined to repeat history. Remember, it's your canvas and your paints. You are the artist in control.

What are some of the choices your birthparents made that you may not?

Having early sex. Whether or not you become sexually active while a teenager is your choice and yours alone. There is no gene, handed down from birthparent to child, that determines when someone should have sex. If your birthparents were teenagers when you were born, it doesn't mean that you were meant to have sex early, too.

You may think that these facts are obvious. Would it surprise you to learn that many adopted children whose birthparents were teenagers do have sex at an early age? Psychologists who have talked with these young people say that many of them feel a strong pull toward imitating the behavior of their birthparents. Somehow the adoptee may feel that doing so will bring her closer to her birthmother, someone who, for now, remains out of reach.

If you are having thoughts along these lines, it's important that you talk with a trusted adult. If you feel you cannot talk to a parent, then find a teacher, school counselor, coach, minister, or aunt or uncle whom you can confide in.

Hopefully you will wait until you are much older to have sex. But whenever you make the decision, it should not be because you feel forced into having sex based on your birthparents' history.

Dropping out of school. Danny was sixteen when he told his mother he wanted to drop out of high school. "My birthparents didn't finish high school," he explained. "I don't want to either."

Of course, Danny didn't know for sure that his teenage birthparents remained high school dropouts. They may have gone back to school after he was born. But Danny, who was struggling in school, wanted to use this information to back up his own desire to quit school.

Fortunately, his parents didn't go along with his plan. Rather than allowing him to drop out, they arranged for him to get some extra help in school. Danny is now in college and doing fine.

Of course, not all birthparents are high school dropouts. Sarah Saffian discovered that both of her birthparents were college graduates. Tim Green, who is a former professional football player, wrote *A Man and His Mother: An Adopted Son's Search*. He discovered that his birthmother was a teacher and that his birthfather was very wealthy, having started up his own computer software company.

Whatever you may learn about your birthparents, their successes or failures are theirs, not yours. If you find out that your birthparents went to technical school, it doesn't mean you can't go to a liberal arts college, or vice versa. If your parents were teachers, it doesn't mean that you can't be a police officer or a carpenter. You may have inherited certain talents and abilities from them. But what you do with those skills is your decision and only yours.

SUCCEEDING AGAINST ALL ODDS

In 1993, Faith Daniels had it all—looks, talent, fame, and love. At thirty-five, she was happily married with two children. She also had reached the top of her profession in broadcast journalism, sitting in as anchor of the NBC weekend evening news and hosting an NBC talk show.

One of her talk shows dealt with a heavy topic: women who had become pregnant after being raped. Daniels listened while her two female guests talked about their experiences. One had decided to terminate the pregnancy, while the other chose to have the baby. Just before Daniels cut to a commercial, she made a comment that stunned her guests and audience alike: she was the product of a rape.

"There are many adoptees—including this one—who were conceived in the exact same way (through rape)," Daniels said, her voice trembling slightly. "It doesn't really matter how you were conceived. Only what you've become."

Daniels had always known that a New Jersey couple had adopted her when she was eight months old. But it was only in 1985, when she was twenty-seven, that she learned her birthmother, then seventeen, had become pregnant after being beaten and raped by a young man she was dating.

"Date rape is truly an awful thing," Daniels said. "But if a child is the result, and is placed in a loving home, there should be no stigma."

Daniels' experience illustrates that no person, adopted or otherwise, should let the circumstances surrounding their birth hold them back. Daniels had always thought that the nuns in the Catholic orphanage had named her Faith. Later she discovered that her birthmother had given her that name, knowing that she would need faith in herself and others to realize her potential.

A BIRTHMOTHER'S WISH FOR HER SON

The one thing you should know about your birthparents, particularly your birthmother, is that deciding for adoption was a decision made with a lot of thought and care. They wanted you to live to enjoy a full and happy life. Don't ever feel guilty or disloyal to them because you have embraced your adoptive family. That is exactly what they hoped would happen.

Listen to one birthmother who expressed these

feelings so well to the couple adopting her two-day-old son:

"I am calling him Moses because he lives—twice I scheduled abortion appointments and decided it wasn't his fault or folly that he'd been conceived...and I knew he'd be beautiful, healthy and in some way, a very welcome addition to this earth. I feel like I am placing Moses in his reed basket and sailing him down the Nile—his Nile, your Nile—mine....Please let him know that he was given out of love; he was conceived in love and I feel so good and sure that your love is now what he mostly needs."

CHAPTER THREE
I'm Different from My Adoptive Parents— It Must Be Because I'm Adopted

"My parents never listen to me. They just assume they have all the facts and I don't. I really have nothing in common with them. I am nothing like my mother. She is so serious. I just like hanging out with my friends— having a good time."

"My parents won't let me date. All my friends are allowed to go to the movies with boys. Why are they treating me this way? They obviously never felt like I do when they were my age. We are so different."

"I'm so unlike my parents. I can't stand their music and they hate mine. They are always nagging me about the way I dress. How did I end up in this family?"

Have you ever felt like these teens? Does it seem that you and your parents no longer communicate? That you seem to come from different planets?

Do you ever think that the reason you and your parents are so different has to do with your adoption?

Along with fantasizing about who your birthparents are, you probably fantasize about how your birthparents would relate to you. Your biological parents would understand you better, listen to you, let you date, enjoy your music, and compliment you on your clothing choices.

Wrong!

Would it surprise you to learn that all of the kids quoted above live with their biological parents? None was adopted. And yet these teens, like you, believe they have nothing in common with their parents. So, if you are feeling disconnected from your family, perhaps what you are experiencing is adolescence, not adoption.

All parents—biological and adoptive—hope to protect their children from dangers. Older and hopefully wiser, parents look at the world through more experienced eyes. What they once considered "cool"—ignoring curfews, wearing certain clothes, and drinking or using drugs—no longer seems fun. When they think of their children doing some of the things they may have done, they get frightened. They survived all right. But what if their children aren't so lucky?

When you were younger, you appreciated your parents' efforts to shield you from harm. You didn't mind having your mom stand underneath while you struggled to reach the top of the jungle gym. When you tried to ride your new two-wheeler, it was comforting to have your dad run alongside, ready to stop you from falling.

Now that you are a teen, however, you are eager to be independent and explore on your own. And you are apt to resent your parents whenever they try to stop you. It's easy to see why parents and teenagers—all teenagers, adopted or not—often end up on opposing sides.

In this chapter, we are going to talk about your adoptive parents. And you need to take it on faith, even if you don't believe it, that your parents do understand a lot of what you feel. Even though there's no biological connection, you do have a lot in common. That's because so many feelings and experiences are universal ones—even down to the feeling of being misunderstood and different from everyone else in your family.

There are also advantages to having your adoptive parents around even if they are driving you nuts. Unlike your birthparents, your adoptive parents are available. You can talk with them about all sorts of things, and about your adoption in particular. Are you afraid to bring up the subject of adoption? You shouldn't be. This chapter will give you some ideas on starting a conversation with your parents so that you can learn more about your origins and your adoption without feeling uncomfortable.

Remember that you are not going through adoption alone. Your parents are also part of the experience. While adoption has brought much joy to everyone in your family, naturally there are sad and difficult times, too, for your parents as well as for you. Learning to share the bad times as well as the good ones will bring everyone closer together and make your entire family stronger.

ADOPTION AND ADOLESCENCE

All teens—adopted and nonadopted—go through the process of separating from their parents. That's what growing up is all about, becoming independent so that you can lead your own life. But this breaking away can be painful as parents and teens adjust to a new relationship.

During adolescence, roughly the years from ten through nineteen, kids go through many developmental stages. You are already noticing some of these changes. You are growing physically. During puberty, when children begin to develop sexually, girls and boys can grow twenty inches taller and add anywhere from twenty to thirty pounds to their frame.

Those are the changes you can see. But there are other transformations going on inside of you that you can't see. These affect how you think and feel. The way you reason also is becoming more sophisticated. (That's one of the reasons why you are now giving more thought to your adoption.) You are able to ponder complex questions for longer periods of time. You can begin to analyze many of the events occurring around you. Your schoolwork is becoming more challenging because your teachers know you can now handle this harder kind of work.

You also are undergoing many emotional changes. You feel things more deeply now as an adolescent. And you are beginning to attach words to these feelings. You can explain to someone when and why you are feeling sad, angry, hurt, happy, or scared. Have you felt the first stirrings of love? Those feelings may be uncomfortable at times—wonderful, scary, mystifying, all of the above—and what you are going through is normal.

As you begin to develop physically and emotionally, you begin to see yourself more as an individual and less as an addition to your parents. You no longer like the same things your parents like. You are acquiring your own tastes in music, clothing, foods, movies, even friends. You want to become more independent. You have taken the first steps on the path to adulthood. This pulling-away process is normal—for all teens, non-adopted and adopted.

As you feel yourself growing apart from your parents, you wonder why this is happening. You know that you love them and feel close to them. Then why do you seem to be disagreeing and arguing all the time? Why are you always so angry at them? Why don't they understand you? When you look for an explanation, your adoption seems the most obvious answer.

In truth, most teens fight a battle of independence with their parents. But your breaking-away process is more complicated. Knowing ahead of time why this is true, will help you handle the situation better during your teenage years.

DISCOVERING YOUR IDENTITY

An adopted child has a more difficult job because he has two families to size up: his biological family and his adoptive family. A great debate rages in parenting circles, as well as in scientific ones, that can best be summed up as "nature vs. nurture." The question is about what has more influence over children, "nature," their biological roots, or "nurture," how they are raised.

For an adopted child, the answer may turn out to be both. Your genes obviously play a major role in who you are, what you are good at. In the last chapter on birthparents, you learned what you may have inherited from them—talents and interests and, of course, physical resemblance. Here, we are going to talk about what you have taken from your adoptive parents.

Your family environment

From the first day your parents brought you home, they became the center of your life. This was particularly true if you were adopted when you were an infant and never knew another family. During your first few months, you grew to love and depend on your parents because they were taking care of your every need. They fed you when you were hungry, many times getting up in the middle of the night to do so. The way your mother held you, the way your father burped you, all became very familiar and comforting.

As you grew older, your parents began to teach you about the world, its pleasures and its dangers. They introduced you to ice cream, swimming pools, and sleigh rides in the snow. Your father grabbed you just before you placed your hand on that hot stove. When you fell off your trike, your mother was the first one there to pick you up and comfort you.

They taught you to know right from wrong. Sharing your toys with a friend was right; throwing sand in another child's face was wrong. When you began to talk, you learned to say, "Please," and "Thank you," and not to interrupt others when they were talking. Your parents asked you not to call people names and to say, "I'm sorry," when you hurt someone's feelings.

You may not have been aware of all these things while they were happening. But what your parents have been doing all along is teaching you values. By now, these principles are so familiar that you consider them a part of yourself, a part of your identity. Those family values are what you have inherited from your parents, and they hope you will hold onto them as you become an adult.

So who you are is a mix of biological inheritance and everyday life experience. What is the ratio? Nobody knows for sure. Whatever the balance, you are individual and unique. Even biological siblings, who have the same mother and father, are different. If you had a genetic sibling, that person would still be different from you.

Whether adopted or not, people are all interested in their beginnings. Do you remember the TV mini-series *Roots*? It was based on a best-selling book by Alex Haley. It told the story of several generations of African-Americans, beginning with Kunta Kinte, an African who was kidnapped and brought to the U.S. as a slave in the 1700s. The mini-series spawned a nationwide "roots" movement. It no longer seemed enough to know biological parents and grandparents. People of all ages and nationalities traveled to all corners of the world to learn more about their ancestors. Why? Perhaps by learning more about where we came from, what we have inherited, we can better understand and appreciate who we are.

Researching your adoptive roots

The dictionary defines "roots" as "the close ties one has with some place or people through birth or upbringing." That means that you have two sets of roots: those that tie you to your birthfamily and those that bind you to your adoptive family. At some point you might want to research your biological roots. (We'll talk about that in the next chapter.) But before you begin that task, why not start with the here and now by studying your other set of roots, those that anchor you to your adoptive family?

You may think that you know all there is to know about your family. But no one can ever have enough information about their relatives near and far. Learning more about your family can help you discover other things you have in common. You may uncover a long-lost relative that even your parents never knew about.

How do you go about your task? Pretend that you have been assigned to write an article about your family for your school newspaper. How would you prepare to tackle that job?

You might begin by focusing on people, places, and things.

People. Start with the oldest members of your family, your grandparents or great-grandparents, if they are still living. If these family members were born in

another country, ask them to recall for you what their lives there were like. Do they remember their trip to America? What was that journey like? You may discover that an older relative has a vivid memory of an important event in history that you have studied in school.

Do some research on your parents. Talk with grandparents, aunts, and uncles. What were they like as children? Teenagers? Was your mother a Beatles maniac? Was your father consumed with becoming a major-league baseball player? What special things will you discover that can help you better understand your parents?

Parents who have biological children often talk about the mother's pregnancy and the scene in the delivery room when the baby was born. Find out what your parents did while they waited to adopt you. What were they doing when they received the call telling them they were about to become parents? Whom did they tell? How did they celebrate? How did they feel when they saw you for the first time?

Places. Along the way, ask your relatives to describe places that have special memories for them. Can you visit the neighborhood where your parents grew up? How is it different from your own? When you were an infant, did your family live in a different house? Do you remember what it looked like?

Where did your parents take you when you were a

baby? What were the parks, playgrounds, museums, and restaurants they took you to? Plan a day revisiting some of these places. Encourage your parents to describe some of these outings. These are all parts of your history.

Things. Most parents keep special mementos—photographs, scrapbooks, baby books, clothes, rattles—from their children's early days. Some of these items may be on display in your living room or den. Others may have been put away so that you can give them to your own children someday. Ask your parents if you can see them again, and look for details you might have missed. Does your baby book record special milestones in your life— when you took your first step, said your first word? Do your parents remember how they felt when these events occurred?

Photo albums can help you relive special times. Test your memory. Do you remember your first ride on a roller coaster? The vacation to Florida? Your first lost tooth? Have your parents kept any special toys, a stuffed dog or a worn blanket that you carried with you everywhere? Can you look through old school papers, crayon drawings, finger paintings, that your parents have tucked away?

What will you learn from this research project? You will see that, through your adoption, you are part of a family chain that is every bit as strong as your genetic one. You may not have your father's chin or your mother's eyes, but you have inherited their spirit. You can duplicate your family rituals—special celebrations at holidays or just something as simple as reading a story together before bedtime—one day with your own family.

SOME OF YOUR FAVORITE THINGS

Families are all about sharing. Rather than focus on ways you are different from your parents, look for ways that you are alike:

Hobbies. People don't have to be related biologically to share the same interests. When you live with someone who enjoys a particular hobby or activity, it's easy to get caught up in that enthusiasm. A husband who enjoys tennis may teach his wife the sport so that they can play together. One friend may turn another friend on to bowling, fly fishing, quilting, snowboarding, or gardening.

In the same way, parents can share their hobbies and interests with their children. That may already have happened. Are there activities you have learned to love after doing them with your parents? From your father you may have learned the joy of cooking, either helping him bake bread or barbecue in the backyard. Was your mother's gift to you her love of books?

One adoptive mother tells this story: "I have always loved to read and hoped to pass that passion on to my daughter. Whenever we took a bus or a train, I would encourage her to take along a book. There we would sit, reading side by side. Today she is an avid reader and

I hope I can take just a little credit for that."

Mannerisms. After people live together for long periods of time, they pick up some of the same expressions and habits. Sarah Saffian often thought about the similarities between herself and her adoptive father. They both were enthusiastic talkers, using lots of hand gestures and lively facial expressions to get their points across.

People often joke about married couples developing the same habits—tapping a pencil or chewing a lip while thinking. But the same magic can happen between a parent and child, as it did with Saffian and her father.

ADOPTION AND YOUR PARENTS

Hopefully, you and your parents have always been able to talk about how you came to be part of your family. In fact, many adopted children, when asked, can't really remember when they first began to learn about their adoption. "I've always known I was adopted and have always felt I could talk about it with my parents," said Marcy, sixteen.

Adoption experts teach parents to consider the child's age. With a child who is in kindergarten, parents often keep the story very simple: "Your birthparents couldn't take care of you and so the agency found us and we became your parents." As the child grows older, the parents can add more information.

You may find that you go through long periods of time when neither you nor your parents mention adoption. "My youngest daughter seems uninterested in talking about adoption even though I am very open," said one adoptive mother of two daughters. "I am surprised that she doesn't ask more!" This often happens right around middle school, when you are busy with so many activities that adoption is the last thing on your list.

Yet one day you may be suddenly consumed by curiosity and have many questions. Your parents probably know more about your adoption than they have told you. After all, you are older now and there are perhaps more details you have yet to learn. But you are reluctant to begin the discussion. Why?

I worry about hurting my parents' feelings if I ask about my birthparents.

You aren't alone. Many adoptees have this concern. Do you worry that your parents will think that you are trying to replace them? That they might feel threatened with the reminder that you have another set of parents?

"I never really talk to my parents about my adoption because I don't want to hurt their feelings," said Ashley, seventeen. "I don't know if they would be uncomfortable if I asked them about it, because I've never tried. I do talk to my friends, though. They are understanding and I know they won't be hurt no matter what I tell them—not like my parents."

Your parents are stronger than you think. Like most adoptive parents, yours have probably had to deal with the fact that they couldn't have children biologically. This infertility battle more than likely went on for many years. One or both of your parents may have had to undergo medical tests—time-consuming and sometimes painful ones. They had to deal with their feelings, possibly talking with a doctor or a psychologist.

If you were adopted through an agency, your parents had to answer many questions during their home study. They were asked about their attitude toward your birthparents. (One social worker said that she doesn't approve anyone who has negative feelings toward birthparents.) The social worker told them that at some point in the future you would ask about your birthparents. If the social worker was thorough, she explained to your parents why it was important for you to learn about your birthparents. And she probably reassured them that your asking wouldn't change your feelings towards them. So most likely, your parents expect that you will have questions and want information.

Will my parents understand why I need to learn about my birthparents?

Remember that the fact that you're adopted has touched your parents' lives, too, in a major way. Even before you could talk, other people were asking your parents about your adoption. They had to learn how to handle people who became too inquisitive or made insensitive remarks. So that they could speak honestly and knowledgeably about adoption, they probably took steps to educate themselves. Perhaps they have been reading books about adoption ever since you were a baby. They may belong to an adoptive-parent group where they can talk with others who share their experiences.

This education process has been a gradual one for your parents. They have had many years to sift through papers, research, and speeches.

Most studies about adoption reach the same conclusion: adoptees who learn about their origins have an easier time forming an identity. Your parents more than likely understand this fact and will be ready to answer your questions.

My parents say they don't have much information.

It may not be your parents' fault that they have so little to tell you. Some adoptive parents receive a lot of information about the birthparents, while others receive almost none. How much information your parents have depends upon how you were adopted.

In a *confidential* or *closed adoption*, the birthmother and the adoptive parents do not meet and don't know each other's names or addresses. Each side receives only non-identifying information about the other side—the general area where they live, their professions, ethnic background, health problems, and possibly hobbies. If your adoption was a confidential one, then your parents probably know very little about your birthparents.

Most foreign adoptions are confidential ones. Unfortunately, in many foreign countries, there is still a stigma attached to unmarried women who have babies or who, because they cannot take care of them, must surrender them to government agencies. In most cases, the birthmother chooses not to be identified.

If your adoption was a confidential one, the records are sealed and you will not be able to request information until you are eighteen. Even then, depending upon the state where you were adopted, you may not be able to find out about your birthparents without a lot of tough detective work. (More on this in the next chapter.)

If your adoption was *semi-open*, then your birthmother and parents may have met. In this type of adoption, the birthmother actually gives her baby to the adoptive parents. After that, there may be limited contact for a set time through phone calls or letters.

With an *open* adoption, the birthmother and adoptive parents exchange names and addresses and agree to stay in touch. Some birthmothers stay in close contact, while others do not. But because the adoptive parents know the birthmother, they have much more information to pass along to their child.

If you don't have a lot of information, you may find the situation frustrating, particularly if you have a sibling whose adoption was more open. Daria, seventeen, who was born in Korea, said that her sister, Joanna, who was born in Afghanistan, has always known more about her birthparents.

"When I was younger, I was always angry at my sister because she knew so much more about her birthparents," said Daria. "Now that I'm older, I understand more why it happened that way."

What do you do, however, if your parents have information but stonewall you and refuse to answer your questions? Don't give up. You need to make a good argument outlining why you need information about your adoption now. Here are some things you can say to your parents to encourage them to open up:

"I need more information about my adoption now."

You may want to start by explaining why you need more information now. Be honest. Are you wondering what you will look like? Did someone make a comment to you that started you thinking about your birthparents? Did you see a TV show or read something that triggered your curiosity? Perhaps you have no solid reason for asking right now, except that your need to know has grown so great that you can no longer stop yourself from asking.

"My adoption story is my story, and I'm entitled to know it."

Your story didn't begin with your adoption. It began with your birth. Even though there are facts about your birthparents and the circumstances of your birth that your adoptive parents don't know, you are entitled to whatever information they have. Small, insignificant details may have great meaning for you as you begin to record you own story.

"Please don't protect me. I need to know the truth."

Many parents hope to protect their child from hurtful information about the birthparents. Even if your adoption story is not a happy one, eventually you will be better off knowing the truth. In fact, 99.9 percent of adoptees say they would rather know the truth. Tell your parents you need them to be honest with you and to help you understand and deal with anything they tell you. Without knowing your true story, you may imagine circumstances that are far worse.

"I'm not looking for a new set of parents."

Your parents are only human. They may worry about what will happen if you search for and find your birthparents. Will you then reject them as your parents?

Reassure them that they are your true parents, but that you still have a need to learn more about your birthparents.

"Will you go with me to the adoption agency?"

If nothing you say convinces your parents to open up, perhaps you need to enlist some help. If your adoption was handled through an agency, call a social worker there. (If your adoption was independent, you may still find that an agency social worker will help you.) Explain the situation and ask whether you may come in with your parents to discuss your adoption and your need for information. Chances are once this professional talks with your parents, they will change their minds and share more information with you.

Remember, talking with your parents about your adoption should be ongoing—not a one-time event. They would never be able to cover (and you would never be able to absorb) all the information in one sitting. The important thing is to start talking...and then continue talking.

What do you do if, after you've reasoned and pleaded, your parents still won't talk with you about adoption? This situation would be unfortunate, but it doesn't have to mean that you don't talk about adoption. You will just need to find other people who can help you. Can you talk with your grandparents or a favorite aunt or uncle? Maybe they have some information. Maybe they can have a talk with your parents about your needs right now. If you have older siblings who were adopted, they may be able to answer some of your questions as well as give you some guidance for approaching your parents.

You might also want to talk with a favorite teacher or guidance counselor at school. These trained professionals may be able to better explain to your parents why you need to know more about your adoption.

You are now able to have your own opinion on many subjects. Sometimes your opinion may be different from those of your parents. If your parents clam up when you start discussing adoption, that doesn't mean you should stop talking about adoption, too. You may need to find others to talk with. But adoption is part of your life experience, and you have the right to learn more about it.

FITTING TOGETHER THE PIECES

Your parents may be upset that you are moving away from them. They know that you must learn to become more independent and do things on your own, yet it is hard for them to see you needing them less. Ironically, the closer you have been to your parents, the more painful this breaking-away process becomes.

Your teenage years are a time of growth and exploration. Each day you add new pieces to the puzzle which will ultimately become the "adult" you. Many people have affected who you are, but your adoptive parents have no doubt played an important (if not the most important) role. They were not responsible for

bringing you into this world, but they have been the ones walking alongside you all these years, loving you, caring for you, guiding you, and teaching you.

Think about the Superman story. The Man of Steel inherited his supernatural powers from his birthparents, but his adoptive parents were the ones who kept him grounded. They gave him the roots that allowed him to soar.

CHAPTER FOUR
Should I Search for My Birthparents?

When you think about your birthparents, do you imagine searching for them? Do you imagine actually finding them?

If you are like most adopted teens, you have both a "wish" and a "fear" about searching. You wish you could find your biological family, but you are also afraid of what you would find. You wish your birthmother would want you back, but you are also afraid that she would want you back.

Sound a little crazy? It's not. The fear of the unknown often stops us in our tracks, even though we may desperately want the answers to our questions. That's probably why only a small number of adopted people actually do complete their searches, though many think about it and many others begin but never finish.

It's not easy to search. With closed or confidential adoptions, much of the information is sealed. In some states you can ask for this information when you become an adult, usually when you turn eighteen. But some states are more strict and deny even adults access to their birth records.

Even though you are probably too young to begin

a search now, that doesn't mean that you don't think about searching. Why do adopted people search? What are good reasons, and not-so-good reasons, for seeking biological parents? What role should your parents play? What are the laws about searching? Must searching always end in a meeting?

Young people feel differently about searching. "I sort of have these images in my mind," said Jane, seventeen. "Searching and finding my birthparents would ruin all that."

"Maybe I'll see my birthparents in heaven," said Scott, twelve. "But I don't think about meeting them here on earth."

"Meeting my birthparents, seeing their faces—that's all I ever think of," said Robin, fourteen. "I imagine that they will be excited to see me."

"I'm an only child," said Whitney, thirteen. "So I always wonder if I have other brothers and sisters. That would be neat."

If you hunger for more information about your birthparents, there are additional ways to satisfy that need now, without actually searching. We will talk about other options you have, like learning as much as you can by talking to people who were a part of your adoption.

WHY DO ADOPTEES SEARCH?

Adopted people have many different explanations for wanting to search. Perhaps your reasons will be included in this list, or you may have other thoughts.

Curiosity

Curiosity tops the list of why people search. Sometimes that curiosity is easily satisfied, particularly at a young age. "I just want to know my birthmother's name," said Elizabeth, eleven, who went away happily after learning the answer (Maria) from her mother.

Older teens may want more information. "I never think about what it would be like if I wasn't adopted," said Ashley, seventeen. "But I've always kind of wondered where I came from, what my roots are, who my actual mother and father are."

Sometimes curiosity is sparked through a comment made by another adopted teen. "I was in my theology class and one of my classmates started talking about how her adoption made her feel," said a seventeen-year-old. "It was a total click. I had never thought about my adoption as a big deal, but after that I did begin to wonder."

Most adoption stories only include what the birthparents were doing when the child was born. As a result, birthparents may become frozen in time. Updating the story allows an adopted person to "unfreeze" that early image. "I always think of my birthparents as being fifteen and sixteen," said Aaron, fifteen. "I have to keep reminding myself that they are now thirty and thirty-one and have gotten on with their lives."

Even though most teens know why they were adopted, they still would like to hear their birthparents' explanation. "I wouldn't ask my birthparents if they loved me," said one adopted girl. "I'm pretty sure they did. But I would like to know why they decided to give me up, and to learn what they are doing now."

Teens also want to know whether their birthparents have forgotten them. "I wonder if my birthparents think about me," said Diana, sixteen.

Reassuring Birthparents They Did the Right Thing

When the Search Institute did its study on adoption, the researchers asked teens why they wanted to meet their birthparents. A large number wanted to tell their birthparents that they were happy and glad to be alive. "I have had a much better life than I would have had if I had remained in Korea," said one girl.

Another agreed. "I am happier where I am because, who knows?" said a girl who was born in South America. "If I had stayed with my birthmother, I might be struggling and hungry somewhere. Right now, I go to a great school, have two parents who love me, and have a good life. If things hadn't turned out so well, then I think I'd be more resentful."

When Tim Green met his birthmother, he assured her that she had done the right thing. "Everything worked out just the way it should have. I couldn't be happier," he told his birthmother in one of their early phone conversations. "I've had a great life. Look where I am. Look at all the things I've been able to do. Everything was made possible, only because of the decision that you made...."

Jessica, seventeen, echoed Tim's feelings. "I want to say thank you to my birthparents," she said. "They gave me life. They gave me to a family that loves me, wants to be with me, and cares for me."

Adopted teens understand that adoption is not always the easiest solution. "My birthmother didn't take the cowardly way out, going to a doctor and getting rid of me very fast," said Jessica. "It was a difficult thing to have me and give me up."

Life-Changing Event

Many adopted teens develop the desire to search when they experience a family crisis, such as the death of an adoptive parent or the divorce of their parents. This reaction is easy to understand. When your immediate world seems to be coming apart through death or divorce, it's natural to want to replace the structure that was once there. Fantasizing about a ready-made biological family can be tempting.

Tense times in the family may also push an adopted teen toward searching. And tense times often occur more frequently now that you're older and naturally wanting to break away from your family. And this is happening just when you're growing more curious.

"You always think about it when you're having a fight with your parents," said one teen. "I think about how my birthparents would react. Not to silly things, like, they'd never make me eat asparagus, but about how we'd get along."

You've heard the old saying, "Be careful what you wish for, you just might get it." Sometimes we think that if our wish were granted, all our troubles would disappear. Solving problems, however, is never that simple. There are no quick fixes in our complicated lives. If you are not getting along with your parents, you might be tempted to think that finding your birthparents would help. In reality, that discovery would probably just make your life more difficult. It's probably better to try to work out things with your adoptive parents *before* you bring your birthparents into your life.

Whenever you find yourself fantasizing about your birthparents, stop and think. What triggered the fantasy? If an argument with your parents was the trigger, you will know you are using your birthparents as an escape. Fantasizing about your roots is fine, but don't use it as a way to avoid dealing with your parents.

Health Information

Scientists now know that many illnesses—certain types of cancer, diabetes, high blood pressure—are hereditary. Knowing your medical history—what runs in your family—can alert you to possible health problems. In the past, many adopted people received only sketchy details about the diseases in their biological families. That lack of information has placed many people at risk. These days, in open and semi-open adoptions, adoptive parents receive much more health information about the baby. Even in confidential adoptions handled by agencies, birthparents are asked to fill out lengthy health forms which include a genetic worksheet listing conditions that the child may have inherited.

Young people often take their good health for granted. Only when sickness strikes, will an adopted teen realize she is at a disadvantage. That's what happened to Erica and what caused her to begin actively hunting for her birthparents. At sixteen, she was frequently depressed. After visiting many doctors, she was finally told she is a manic depressive. That means that her moods fluctuate between high highs and low lows. When she is "manic," she has bundles of energy,

dashing around from one activity to the next, unable to sit still even. She is so "up" that she may even go days without sleep. In her "depressive" mood, she is just the opposite. She may cry constantly, lose interest in all her activities, and feel so totally exhausted that she can't get out of bed.

Fortunately, her condition can be controlled with medication. But Erica feels that knowing more about her birthparents would help her better prepare for what may lie ahead as she gets older. "I want to know what else is going on in my family's bloodline that I should be aware of," she said.

While it may seem sensible that an adopted person should be able to find out about his or her biological family's health history, with a confidential adoption, those records are sealed. Say there was a medical emergency. How would an adopted person gain access to those records?

He or she would have to ask the courts for permission to see the records. Usually, the judge would give permission. Even without an emergency, however, you may be able to obtain an updated medical profile of your birthparents. Many states have what is called a medical registry where birthparents can file updates on their medical conditions. An adopted person who also filed would be able to get this information. You don't have to be eighteen to use this system, but your parents would have to sign papers. For more information, have your parents call the health department in the state where your adoption was finalized.

LAWS ABOUT SEARCHING

Different states have different laws about obtaining adoption information that has been locked away. What follows is a rundown of how most states operate. (Laws sometimes change, so you will need to check with the state where your adoption was finalized for the most up-to-date information.)

State registries. Some states have a system called an adoption registry. This is how it works: If you are eighteen and want to be contacted, you register with a specific state agency, usually a social services department. If your birthmother or birthfather also wants to call or meet you and takes steps to register, then someone from the agency will get in touch with you. Identifying information is then given to both you and your birthparent. You are then free to contact each other.

States which have registries include Arkansas, California, Colorado, Connecticut, Florida, Georgia, Hawaii, Illinois, Indiana, Louisiana, Maine, Maryland, Michigan, Missouri, Nevada, New York, Ohio, Oklahoma, Oregon, Pennsylvania, Rhode Island, South Carolina, South Dakota, Tennessee, Texas, Utah, Vermont, West Virginia, and Wisconsin.

Besides state registries, there are others. The International Soundex Reunion Registry in Carson City, Nevada has helped thousands of adopted adults and birthparents locate each other. The Internet has

given rise to several registries. Perhaps you have even run across some of these listings when you've been online. While state registries and the one in Nevada require adopted people be at least eighteen, there are no such restrictions on the Internet.

Confidential intermediary. Again, you must be at least eighteen to use this system. Here's how it works: An adopted adult would contact the confidential intermediary for his state and ask to receive information on a birthparent. The confidential intermediary, who would have access to identifying information, would use that information to locate and contact the birthparent. If the birthparent agrees, the adoptee would be given the information which could actually include the names and addresses of the birthparents.

States which have confidential intermediaries include Arizona, Colorado, Illinois, Michigan, Minnesota, North Dakota, Oklahoma, Vermont, Wisconsin, and Wyoming.

Open records. A few states actually will hand over information to an adult adoptee who asks. These states include Alaska, Kansas, and Tennessee.

As you can see, most states have laws that say you must be at least eighteen to retrieve information that has been locked away about your adoption. Why should you have to wait? Don't you have a right to this information right now? After all, you are the one who was adopted, right?

That's true, but, as you have learned in the other chapters, you are not the only one involved in your adoption. Your birthparents and your adoptive parents are involved, too. Some of these laws were passed to protect their privacy.

Searching by adopted people is a controversial issue. Many adopted adults believe that they are entitled to know the identity of their birthmothers, even if the birthmother has requested privacy. These adopted adults have won some important legal battles. In at least three states—Alaska, Kansas, and Tennessee—adopted adults may now obtain their original birth certificates with the names of their biological parents.

In all other states, getting your original birth certificate is no easy task. When she was sixteen, Jessica  was determined to find hers. She went to the public library in her city taking with her the birth certificate listing her adoptive parents' names. There are numbers at the top of the birth certificate, and Jessica knew that those numbers would match the ones on her original birth certificate. She also knew where and when she was born. Still, she found that there had been thousands of births on that day in her city. She was forced to plow through all of them. Finally, she found a match. She learned the names of her birthparents, although she will still have to wait until she is eighteen to get any more information.

"I was so excited, I flew out of the library," she said. Right now, Jessica does not plan to search further. While her parents were supportive, they feel she should pay to continue the search, something that could run into a lot of money if she needs to hire a private investigator to find her birthparents. She will not be able to afford a search, she says, until she is older and working.

If you are thinking of searching before you are eighteen, a word of caution. Searching is a serious decision that should never be made without careful thought. Once you have found a birthparent and exchanged information about who you are and where you live, there is no turning back. Your birthmother or birthfather may become a part of your life, even if you later decide you don't want that. That is why most states have laws restricting the release of information until the adopted person is mature enough to handle what might follow.

Searching should not be a spur-of-the-moment decision. Give yourself time to think through all possible scenarios. Play the "what if" game. For example: "What if I find my birthmother and she rejects me. How would I feel?"

Make a list of all the reasons for finding your birth-parents now and all the reasons for waiting. Do the reasons for searching now really outweigh the reasons for waiting?

Talk with some adolescents who have searched. To locate them, call an adoption agency and ask for a teen support group. You might want to participate in one of their discussions to learn more about searching.

The decision to search is one that should be made after careful thought. No one is saying that you should never search. But perhaps putting it off for awhile might be the best decision.

WHY DO YOU WANT TO SEARCH?

Don't feel guilty if you think about searching for your birthparents. Most adopted people who decide to search do so not because they are unhappy with their families, but because they are curious about their origins. "My daughter, who is seventeen, would tell you that she doesn't feel complete not knowing who her birthparents are," said one adoptive mother who has supported her daughter's efforts by helping her obtain information from the adoption agency.

Also, don't feel there is something wrong with you if you have no desire to search. Kara, who traveled to Korea when she was fifteen, wanted to see the country where she was born. She met with the woman who had taken care of her as a baby, but she had no desire to seek out her birthparents. "I wondered about them a lot more when I was younger," she said. Even finding out that she had siblings living in Korea didn't change her mind.

Searching, however, can mean many different things, as these two examples show. For one girl, searching means finding her birthparents. For another, searching means exploring her native land.

Here are some questions for you to consider:

- *When you think about searching, how do you define it?*
- *What is it that you want to find out?*
- *How much information do you need to satisfy your curiosity?*
- *Are you curious because you don't have enough basic information about your adoption?*
- *If you want to know what your birthparents look like, would you be satisfied with a photograph?*
- *When you think about meeting your birthparents, what do you hope to get out of it?*
- *Do you just want answers to some of your questions or are you hoping to have a real relationship with your birthparents?*

ALTERNATIVES TO SEARCHING

Legally, you are not old enough to go through a full-fledged search, but if you have a growing curiosity to learn more about your background, don't be frustrated. There are ways that you can find out more without actually launching a full-scale hunt. In this section we will discuss some alternatives to searching. You may come up with other ways on your own to help you understand your adoption.

Background information from your parents

Use the information in Chapter Three to get your parents talking. Some facts that were not written down, may be stored in your parents' memories.

Are there papers that they have tucked away for that time when you are old enough to know the truth? A letter your birthmother may have written to you? A blanket she may have knitted for you? Perhaps now is the time for you to receive these items.

For example, Ashley says that when she was eight, her parents showed her a packet of information about her birthparents. At ten, she asked for and received her own copy. "I do look at it from time to time," she says. Through looking at the information, Ashley has learned that her birthparents were both college students and loved outdoor activities, and that her birthmother was musically talented.

One adoptive mother said that she and her husband met her daughter's birthparents, as well as some extended family members, at the time of the adoption. "I have pictures and a video I took of them at the time of the adoption," she said. "I also have a few more pictures they sent me later on." Her daughter has already seen the video once and looked at the pictures. "I don't want my daughter to feel that her adoption is some great mystery or secret," the mother said.

Enlist your parents' help for the next step: talking to others involved in your adoption. Most adoption agencies will not give information to anyone under eighteen without the permission of the parents, so your parents will need to pave the way by calling ahead.

Obtaining non-identifying information

Non-identifying information can help you learn more about your birthparents without actually finding out who they are. Who has these facts? Anyone who was involved with your adoption—adoption-agency officials, lawyers, social workers, hospital workers.

If your adoption was handled through an agency, start with someone there. What information does the agency have about your birthparents? Although as many as seventeen years may have passed since you were adopted, the staff may not have changed that much. You may be lucky enough to locate the social worker who worked with your birthmother. Perhaps you can go through the written material with the social worker and ask questions to fill in some of the gaps.

Perhaps your adoption was handled by an attorney. In most cases, the attorney representing the adopting couple doesn't meet the birthparent, but he or she may still remember tidbits passed along during phone conversations with your birthmother's lawyer. Get any of this information that you can.

While non-identifying information won't help you locate your birthparents, you can still learn a great deal. If your hunt doesn't turn up any photographs, see if you can sketch an image (either mentally or on paper) of what one or both of your birthparents would look like now.

Join a support group of teen adoptees

Searching can sometimes be a frustrating journey. Talking can help you sort out your feelings. And who better to talk with than other teens in the same situation as you? Of course, you may have friends who also were adopted and with whom you can share your thoughts. But a better idea is to find a teen support group run by an adoption agency. These talks will be guided by a skilled social worker. Besides keeping the discussion on

track, the social worker can make sure that anyone who is obviously upset receives follow-up counseling.

If your adoption was handled through an agency, ask if it sponsors a group. If your adoption was handled through an adoption attorney, ask if he or she knows of a group you can join. You can also look in the Yellow Pages for adoption agencies in your area. Ask your school guidance counselor if he or she knows about teen groups, or go to your local library. The librarian will be able to help you find the appropriate social services agencies.

Explore your ethnic heritage

Kara explored her ethnic roots by visiting her native country, Korea. If you were born in a foreign country but won't have the chance to travel there any time soon, there are other ways to learn about your nationality.

An adoption agency that handles many foreign adoptions may sponsor ethnic support groups. Social events that showcase different ethnic groups' foods, languages, religions, traditions, customs, and celebrations are held to help keep adoptees in touch with their backgrounds. Brianne, who was born in Korea, often participates in an International Night held annu-

ally at a local adoption agency. "It's a way for me to get into the whole adoption experience," she said. "My parents began taking me to this event when I was very young. Now I not only go, I work during the event and talk with younger children, answering their questions about Korea."

You might want to keep up-to-date on current events in your country of origin. Clip articles of interest to save in a scrapbook. Zero in on the country's outstanding citizens and achievements.

You can cruise the Internet for sites where you may gather more information on your native land. There may be chat rooms where people can share their knowledge. You may meet other adoptees who also are looking to be educated. However, make sure you never give out your real name, address, or phone number to strangers you meet online.

Write letters or keep a journal

After Sarah Saffian's birthparents contacted her, they agreed to put off a reunion until Sarah felt comfortable meeting them. Instead, for three years, Sarah and her birthparents corresponded through letters, often confessing their innermost thoughts on the adoption.

You don't know your birthmother's or birthfather's address. But that doesn't have to stop you from writing to them. Who will read your letters? You! Think about it: You have the opportunity to put into writing everything you would like to tell your birthparents. Also, you are free to imagine how they would respond.

What would you do with these letters? You could put them in a box and reread them from time to time. You might be surprised to see how your feelings change. What you wrote to your birthmother when you were thirteen may not be what you would say at seventeen.

Writing a letter just for yourself is a good exercise because it allows you to get specific about what you want to know as well as what you want to tell your birthparents. Are you angry? Then say so! Do you wonder why they gave you away? Tell them that and ask them to explain. Would you like to reassure them that you are all right? Put that down. Describe what your life is like, who your friends are, what you hope to do when you grow up. Talk about what you are good at doing, what you most enjoy. Do they have similar talents?

After you have written a letter, put it aside for a few days. Then read it fresh, imagining that you are your birthmother. How would you respond? This exercise will help you identify with your birthmother's situation and perhaps better understand why she decided on adoption.

Some adoption agencies who handle international adoptions will mail letters to the foreign agencies. These letters are given to mothers-to-be who are planning to have their babies adopted by families. There is no guarantee that your birthmother will read your specific letter, but you will know that another birthmother has. Maybe your letter will be a real source of comfort for her and make her feel better about her own decision with adoption.

If letter writing doesn't appeal to you, why not keep a journal? Don't get down on yourself if you don't write something every day. Just write when you feel the need to express your emotions, whether you are feeling sad, happy, excited, or lonely. In fact, it is really interesting and helpful to see how often you *do* write in a journal. It will show you how pressing your urge is to find out more about your birth-parents. Have you written every day for a whole year? That would point to a deep and long-held need. Or, over six months, are there just a couple of entries, both of which were written right after a fight with your adoptive parents? Maybe this means your urge to search is based mostly on spur-of-the-moment anger.

SEARCHING AND YOUR ADOPTIVE PARENTS

What role should your parents play in your search? Hopefully, they will share any information they have and answer your questions. Beyond that, you should not expect them to get actively involved. "I have told my daughter that I will be supportive, but that she will need to search on her own," says one adoptive mother. "I would find it hard to be unemotional if I got actively involved and that might influence her actions."

Your parents might get emotional, too, about your searching. Why?

Your parents may worry that your search will turn up bad news. A parent's first instinct is to protect a child. If it looks like your search will end unhappily, your mother or father might be tempted to discourage you. "My mom has some info on my birthparents and always says she will help me find them if I want to, but I also think she is deathly afraid I will," says one adopted boy, who suspects he might uncover painful facts.

During your teen years, when you are trying hard to understand who you are, your parents might feel the last thing you need is to be disappointed by your birthparents.

Your parents worry that your birthparents may reject you. Although there are many stories of happy reunions, some birthparents do not want to be found and refuse to recognize their child. How would you react to this? "I am totally open to the fact that my birthparents might not want to see me," said Jessica. "If I suddenly showed up on their doorstep, they might have a hard time explaining me to their friends." Would you feel the same way? Margaret, sixteen, admitted that she would be crushed. "To be rejected again? That would be tough."

This kind of rejection is bound to be very painful. Your parents hope that the longer you delay your search, the stronger and more mature you will be, and the better able you will be to deal with possible hurt and disappointment.

Your parents worry about being pushed aside. This is a natural feeling on their part, even though most adoptees emphasize that they would not search to replace their parents. "I would never call my birthparents mom and dad," said Jessica. "They are my birthparents, not my parents."

Your search may catch your parents off-balance. They may think they will end up sharing you with your birthparents. In the future, where will you spend holidays? Will you share your deepest thoughts and dreams with your parents or with these new people who have entered your life? Your parents have these worries. "I would hope that if my children find their birthparents, their relationship would be friendly, but with some distance," said the adoptive mother of two daughters. "Hopefully, they will choose to keep in touch with their birthparents, but not make up for lost years."

ADOPTION–THE WHOLE PICTURE

Many adopted people who set out to search for their birthparents are actually searching for themselves. They hope that learning more about their origins will help them understand themselves better. Yet no matter how much information you collect about yourself, you are still the same person you were the day before. You might be amused to discover that you and your birthmother both love peanut butter. But if you didn't find that out, you probably would have continued to love peanut butter anyway.

As the years go by, you will continue to add broad strokes to the canvas of your life. Right now it is filled with all the family, friends, places, and experiences that have colored your life up to this point. Someday you may add other touches that will represent your biological family. When you look at the canvas, sometimes you may focus on a part that represents your adoptive family. At other times, you will zero in on your friends, and at still other times, your birthmother.

But the best view is the one that allows you to take in the entire picture at once. You will discover that your canvas is large enough to hold all the important things in your life. And you will be amazed at how well they fit together.

LOOK WHO WAS ADOPTED

Athletes

Kitty and Peter Carruthers (Olympic skaters)

Eric Dickerson (NFL running back)

Tim Green (NFL player, NBC sports commentators, author)

Scott Hamilton (Olympic skater)

Greg Louganis (Olympic diver)

Dan O'Brien (decathlon world record–holder,

Olympic champion)

Jim Palmer (Baseball Hall of Fame pitcher)

Entertainers

Halle Berry (actress)

Nat King Cole (singer)

Melissa Gilbert (actress)

Debbie Harry (singer)

Art Linkletter (TV personality)

Charlotte Lopez (Miss Teen USA 1993)

Journalists and Writers

Les Brown (motivational speaker)

Faith Daniels (television anchor)

James Michener (author)

Politicians

Senator Robert C. Byrd (D–WV)

Gerald Ford (former president)

Rev. Jesse Jackson (politician)

Jim Lightfoot (former representative from Iowa)

Businesspeople

Steven Jobs (Apple Computer co-founder)

Dave Thomas (founder of Wendy's)

LOOK WHO HAS ADOPTED

Athletes

Kirby Puckett (Minnesota Twins)

Entertainers

Kirstie Alley (actress)

Loni Anderson (actress)

Taurean Blacque (actor)

Tom Cruise (actor)

Jamie Lee Curtis (actress)

Ted Danson (actor)

Mia Farrow (actress)

Louis Gossett Jr. (actor)

David Kelley (TV writer and producer)

Nicole Kidman (actress)

Patti LaBelle (singer)

Ed McMahon (TV personality)

Rosie O'Donnell (talk show host and actress)

Marie Osmond (singer)